**For a different Bob,
who sees life as fun**

About This Book The illustrations for this book were created digitally. This book was edited by Andrea Spooner and designed by Bob Shea. The production was supervised by Erika Schwartz, and the production editor was Jen Graham. The text was set in Avenir, and the display type is Sol.

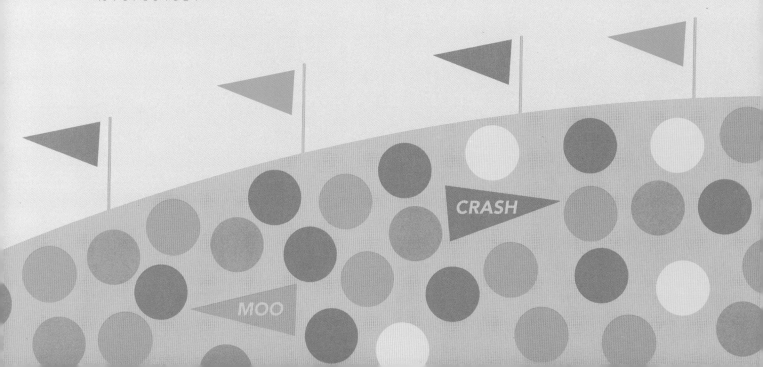

CRASH, SPLASH, OR MOO!

BOB SHEA

SPLASH

LB
Little, Brown and Company
New York • Boston

HOW TO PLAY

Fearless daredevils perform amazing stunts, and YOU guess what happens.

Will they **CRASH?**

Will they **SPLASH?**

Or will they **MOO?**

YAY

Guess right, and win a delicious banana!

Guess ALL the stunts right, and you win the best prize in the world...

Let's meet the team.

First, it's **ACTION CLAM!**
America's favorite splashin', crashin' stunt clam!

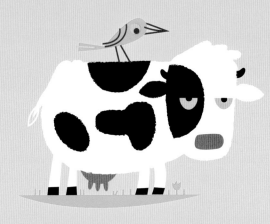

And...this cow!
Who does cow stuff.

And I'm your monkey host,
Mr. McMonkey!

C'mon, let's play!

If *ACTION CLAM...*

drives this **speedy race car...**

into a **giant tower of blocks...**

What do you guess will happen?

Raise your hand if you guess

CRASH!

Raise your hand if you guess

SPLASH!

Raise your hand if you guess

MOO!

VROOOM!

MOO

CRASH

Did you guess CRASH?

**Give yourself a big round
of applause!**

*You just won your
first banana!*

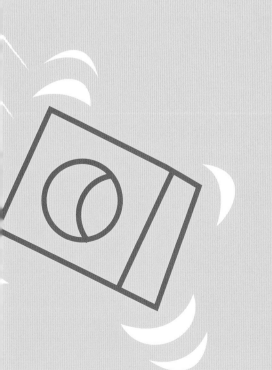

clap!   clap!

clap!   clap!

clap!

clap!

And a super-duper mega-looper!

Okay. For your second banana... can you guess what **amazing thing** is about to happen?

Raise your hand if you guess

CRASH!

Raise your hand if you guess

SPLASH!

Raise your hand if you guess

MOO!

(Psst...it's probably not moo.)

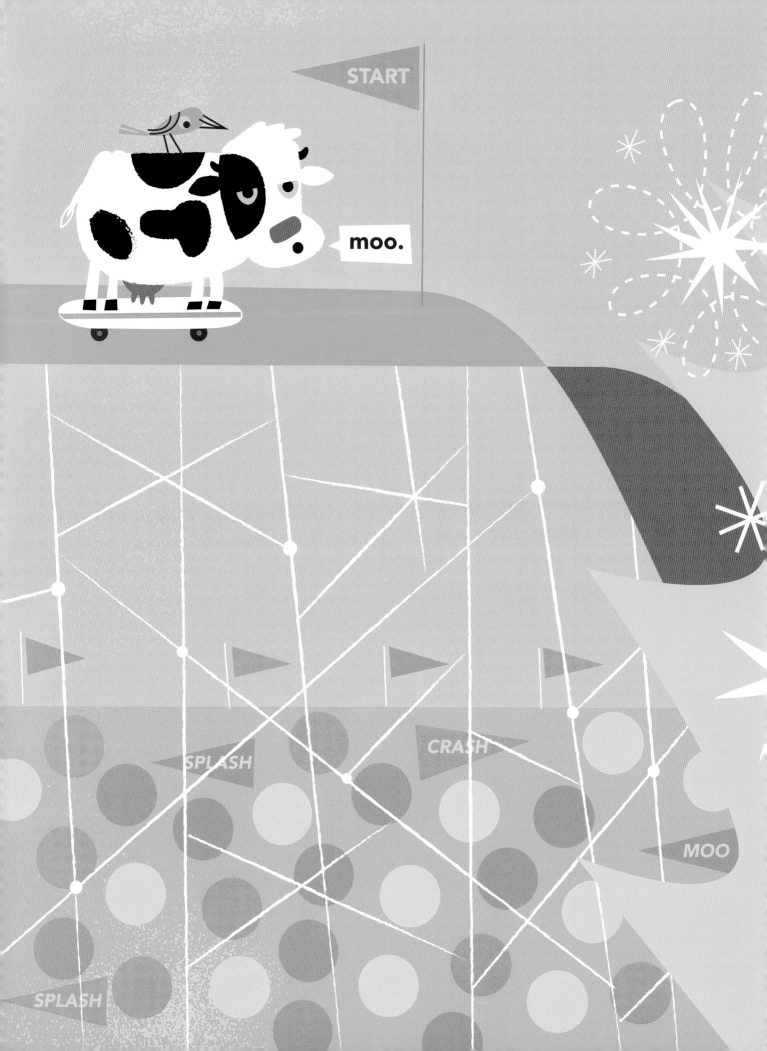

Did you guess **MOO?**

Give yourself a big round of applause!

You win ANOTHER BANANA!

You're a really good guesser!

Okay, Frankie Two-Bananas,
let's see if you can guess
the next one.

and a really faraway glass of water...

For the next sweet treat you eat with your feet, *what do you guess will happen?*

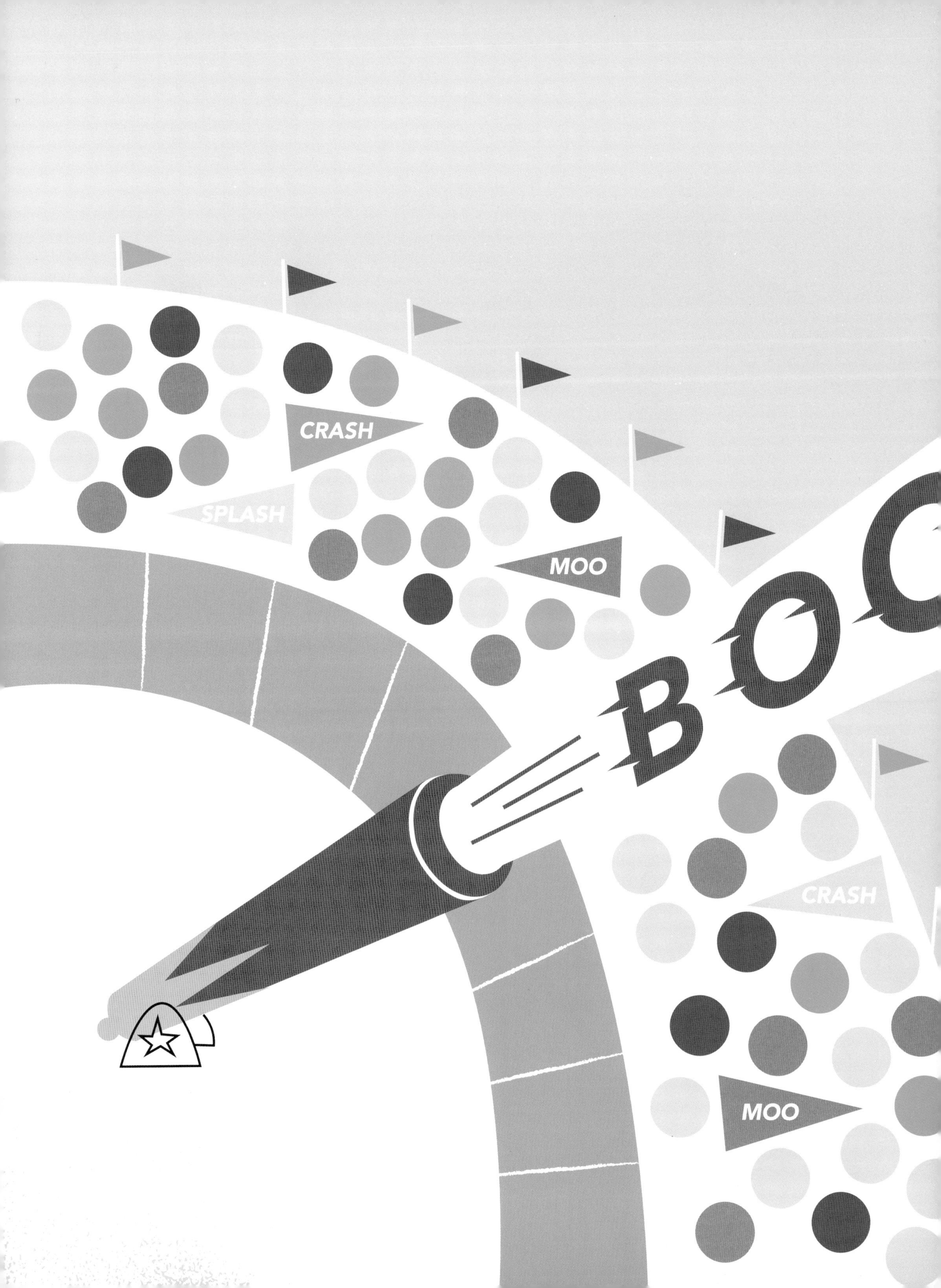
CRASH
SPLASH
MOO
BOO
CRASH
MOO

Raise your hand if you guess

CRASH!

Raise your hand if you guess

SPLASH!

Raise your hand if you guess

MOO!

(I'm guessing MOO, like last time.)

Did you guess SPLASH? Wow! Give yourself a big round of applause!

You win another banana!

Does that make three? That's plenty to share with a banana-lovin' pal. *(Hint, hint.)*

Only one more stunt until

THE BIG ONE!

Cow...

a motorcycle...

and TEN school buses!

Okay, smarty-banana-pants.
What do you guess?

Raise your hand if you guess

CRASH!

Raise your hand if you guess

SPLASH!

Raise your hand if you guess

MOO!

(I guess "HONK!")

MOO????

I did not see that coming!

Did YOU guess MOO?
Give yourself a big round of applause!

You win YET ANOTHER BANANA!

(I'll swing by next week for some banana bread.)

And now, a stunt so big it has an extra-special name.

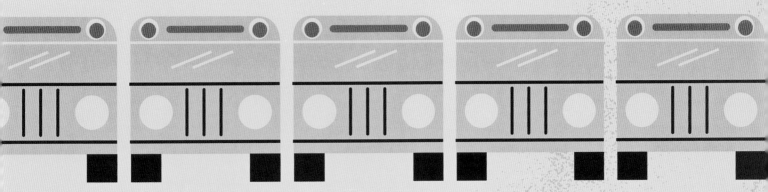

THE
BiG
ONE

This is for the

MOST SECRET, BEST PRIZE
in the whole wide world.

(No pressure.)

Action Clam.
Cow.
A rocket pack.

A piñata.

And a vat of butterscotch pudding.

Raise your hand if you guess CRASH!

Raise your hand if you guess SPLASH!

WHOOSH!

Raise your hand if you guess MOO!

Raise your foot if I can have a BANANA!

SPLASH!

AND...

Did you guess

CRASH, SPLASH, AND MOO?

Give yourself a big round of applause!

Do you know what else that means?

YOU WIN...

THE WORLD'S

BEST PRIZE!

Hold on to your socks,
because they are about to be
KNOCKED OFF!

THAT'S
RIGHT,
YOU WIN...

Here's a big golden-banana round of applause...
for YOU!

**See you next time for more
stunt-guessing
banana-style action!**